Whispers in the Shadows

A Collection of Mysterious Tales

Sayan Panda

Ukiyoto Publishing

All global publishing rights are held by

Ukiyoto Publishing

Published in 2024

Content Copyright © Sayan Panda

ISBN 9789361720062

All rights reserved.
No part of this publication may be reproduced, transmitted, or stored in a retrieval system, in any form by any means, electronic, mechanical, photocopying, recording or otherwise, without the prior permission of the publisher.

The moral rights of the author have been asserted.

This is a work of fiction. Names, characters, businesses, places, events, locales, and incidents are either the products of the author's imagination or used in a fictitious manner. Any resemblance to actual persons, living or dead, or actual events is purely coincidental.

This book is sold subject to the condition that it shall not by way of trade or otherwise, be lent, resold, hired out or otherwise circulated, without the publisher's prior consent, in any form of binding or cover other than that in which it is published.

To the ones who hear them whisper at night.

Contents

The Curious Call	1
The Clock is Ticking	15
The Red Bike	20
The Visions in Sleep	26
The Forgotten Sketchbook	32
The Spare Room Guest	38
About the Author	*43*

The Curious Call

Gunomoy stared at his phone in puzzlement. He had just dialed his own number as a joke, expecting it to ring endlessly in an unresolved loop. But someone had picked up.

"Hello?" came a man's voice through the receiver. It wasn't Gunomoy's voice though. Deep and gravelly, it sent an uneasy chill down his spine.

"Who is this?" Gunomoy asked, his own voice coming out far more shakily than he intended.

A low chuckle sounded from the other end. "The question is, who are you? And how did you get this number?"

Gunomoy's mind raced. This had to be some kind of mistake. Maybe a crossed wire, or a phone stolen with the previous owner's number still attached. "I think there's been a mix up. I dialed my own number by accident."

"And what number is that?"

Gunomoy hesitated, not wanting to give out his information to a stranger. But something told him hanging up now would be a very bad idea. Playing along cautiously, he recited his mobile number.

More chilling laughter. "No, that's not possible. You see, this is my number. And I'm the only one who's ever had it."

A cold sweat broke out on Gunomoy's brow as the implications of that sunk in. This didn't make any rational sense. Before he could respond, the man spoke again.

"Let's play a game. I want to know everything about you, Gunomoy. And you'll find out all about me. Doesn't that sound... fun?" His tone sent unpleasant signals of underlying threat.

Gunomoy almost hung up right then, an intense primal panic rising inside him. But morbid curiosity kept the phone glued to his ear. "What do you want to know?" he asked warily.

"For starters, where are you right now?"

Something told Gunomoy not to reveal that information so readily. He deflected with a question of his own. "What's your name?"

A heavy sigh. "Names are meaningless. But you can call me Siddhartha, since you seem so curious to know. Now, where are you Gunomoy?"

Pausing, Gunomoy glanced around his surroundings, trying to glean any clues without giving too much away. "I'm at home."

"Alone?"

The question sent a chill through him at the implication of being watched, followed. He blinked and peered through the windows, half expecting to see a shadowy figure looking back at him. But there was nothing.

"Yes," he replied, the word catching slightly in his throat.

A thoughtful hum came from Siddhartha. "Pity. I was hoping for a little more... privacy for our game. No matter, we'll find another way. Now, tell me Gunomoy, what are your deepest, darkest secrets? I'm sure you have a few skeletons rattling around in that head of yours."

Gunomoy's heart pounded wildly. Who was this man and how did he seem to know so much? An overwhelming urge to end the call welled up inside him, yet still he hesitated. "I don't have any secrets. And I'm not playing your game."

A humorless chuckle. "Oh, but you already are. The moment you called this number, you became a player whether you wanted to or not. Let's see... I'll bet you've had some naughty thoughts you're not proud of. Dirty little fantasies you've never told a soul."

Revulsion rose in Gunomoy's throat at the insinuation from this complete stranger. Before he could respond, Siddhartha kept prodding eagerly.

"Ooh, or have you done something truly wicked, something even you regret? We all have our demons Gunomoy. I can help you exorcise yours, if only you'd open up to me. I want to know the real you, not the face you show the world."

That was enough. Gunomoy was starting to panic in earnest now. Whoever this Siddhartha was, his intentions seemed far from benign. It was time to end the call, get as far away from this unnerving individual as possible and forget the whole bizarre incident ever happened.

"This conversation is over," Gunomoy said firmly and made to press the button to disconnect. But Siddhartha wasn't finished yet.

"Leaving so soon? But we were just getting to know each other. I'll be seeing you real soon Gunomoy. Then you can tell me all your deepest secrets in person."

Before Gunomoy could respond, the line went dead. He stared at the phone in numb horror, Siddhartha's parting words echoing ominously in his head. Shivers wracked his body as the magnitude of the situation gradually sank in. Who was this man and how had he accessed Gunomoy's private number? More disturbingly, what did he mean by them meeting in person?

In a panic, he scoured every inch of his home checking for any sign of intrusion. But all the doors and windows remained securely locked from the inside. Gunomoy was definitely alone, and yet he had never felt more vulnerable or watched in his life.

The next few days passed in a state of hyper vigilance and insomnia-ridden paranoia for Gunomoy. Every small noise or trick of light had him jumping out of his skin, expecting to turn and find Siddhartha standing right behind him with that mirthless smile. Try as he might, Gunomoy couldn't erase the lingering unease of their disturbing phone call from his mind. Wherever he went, the feeling of being followed and observed by unseen eyes dogged his every step.

After another restless night, Gunomoy dragged himself to the nearest police station in hopes of finding answers, or at least reassurance. But retelling the events only made him feel foolish and paranoid to the skeptical officers. Without any evidence of a tangible threat, there was little they could do except file a report.

"It was probably just a prank call," one officer said dismissively. "I'd forget about it if I were you."

But Gunomoy knew in his gut this ran much deeper than a simple prank. Siddhartha's parting words had hinted at a very real and personal threat. And the suffocating sense of being watched only intensified with each day that passed with no further contact.

After a week with no leads or resolution, Gunomoy began to second guess his own judgment. Perhaps the police were right, and it had merely been a strange coincidence blown out of proportion by an overactive imagination. He started venturing out more in an effort to regain a semblance of normalcy.

One afternoon, Gunomoy decided to chance a coffee at his local hangout, hoping the bustle of people and familiar surroundings would help lift his lingering unease. Settling onto a couch with his steaming latte, he pulled out a book in an attempt to distract from his restless thoughts.

A few pages in, Gunomoy sensed someone standing near. He looked up to find a nondescript man in casual clothes regarding him with a small smile. "Is this seat taken?"

Something about the stranger's mild manner set Gunomoy's nerves instantly on edge. But not wanting to seem rude or paranoid, he gestured for the man to sit. "Go ahead."

"Thanks." The man lowered himself onto the adjacent couch, his posture relaxed yet alert. An amicable silence stretched as Gunomoy tried vainly to focus on his reading once more. Yet he couldn't shake the feeling of intense scrutiny from hisneighbor.

After a few moments, the stranger spoke again in a mild tone. "Rough few days?"

Gunomoy looked up guardedly. Something about the question made it seem loaded with hidden implications. "What makes you say that?"

The man smiled blandly. "You just seem on edge is all. Can't say I blame you after the phone call."

Gunomoy's blood turned to ice in his veins. So this was it, the confrontation he had been dreading. Siddhartha had finally found him, just as promised. But how? Keeping his face rigidly neutral with immense effort, he closed his book slowly and turned to face the man.

"So you're Siddhartha." It wasn't a question.

The man inclined his head casually. "Guilty as charged. It's a pleasure to finally meet you in person, Gunomoy." He extended a hand.

Gunomoy made no move to take it, his mind racing frantically as a million questions swirled. Chief among them was how to get out of this situation safely and quickly. But before he could reply, Siddhartha spoke again in a chummy tone.

"No need to be so on edge, I'm not here to harm you. I simply wanted to continue our little... conversation face to face. You seemed so reluctant to open up over the phone, I thought this more personal setting might help loosen your tongue."

Revulsion and panic warred within Gunomoy as he stared into the placid face of the man who had tormented him.

Gunomoy's mind was blank with terror. All he could focus on was finding a way out of this deadly confrontation. But Siddhartha regarded him pleasantly, as if they were old friends catching up over coffee.

"So now that we're acquainted," Siddhartha continued in a measured tone. "Why don't you tell me something personal? A secret you've never shared with anyone. I think it would be... therapeutic for you."

A cold shower of dread doused Gunomoy's mounting panic. He knew this man would not stop until he had completely unravelled him, one way or another. Desperate for an escape, any escape, Gunomoy made a snap decision.

"I... I once stole money from my parents when I was young," he stammered, grasping for the first innocuous secret that came to mind. "Please, just let me go and I'll tell you whatever you want to know. I won't run, I promise."

Siddhartha regarded him thoughtfully for a long moment, as if weighing the validity of Gunomoy's words. Just when the tension seemed unbearable, he nodded amiably. "Very well, you're free to go for now. But our game has only just begun, Gunomoy. I'll be in touch again real soon."

Without needing further encouragement, Gunomoy shot up from the couch and bolted from the cafe as fast as his legs could carry him. He raced all the way home, locking every possible entrance and hiding in his room like a hunted animal. Gunomoy knew tonight would bring him no sleep, only a fresh terror of the new nightmares Siddhartha was sure to conjure.

His entire world had been plunged into a disturbing hell, and this shadowy man now held complete power over whether Gunomoy would live or die. What deeper secrets would Siddhartha demand next in their sinister game? And how long could Gunomoy keep up this charade before shattering completely under the pressure?

Unbeknownst to him, Siddhartha watched Gunomoy's every panicked movement with a pleased smile. Yes, this new plaything was proving most entertaining indeed. And the real fun had only just begun.

The next few days, Gunomoy barely slept or ate. He checked and re-checked every lock, window and door, constantly peering through curtains for any sign of Siddhartha. But the man remained mysteriously absent.

The endless waiting soon became its own special kind of torment. Gunomoy's anxiety mounted with each passing hour, wondering what new horrors Siddhartha had planned. Why was he drawing this out instead of coming for the kill?

On the fourth night, Gunomoy's phone rang with an unknown number. His heart nearly stopped before answering with clenched dread.

"Hello Gunomoy," came Siddhartha's silky voice. "Are you having fun yet with our little game?"

Gunomoy's throat closed up, rendering him speechless. What could he possibly say to this madman?

Siddhartha took his silence in stride. "Don't worry, I'm not here to hurt you...yet. I simply want to know you, inside and out. For that, we'll need to meet again. Tomorrow afternoon, at the abandoned warehouse off Oak Street. Don't be late!"

The line went dead before Gunomoy could protest. He was trapped in Siddhartha's twisted scheme with no way out. Going to the meet could mean certain death, but not going was its own kind of endless torture.

That night, Gunomoy barely slept at all. When morning came, he sat paralyzed with indecision and fear. As noon approached, he realized with sinking dread that he had no choice. He had to face Siddhartha, if only to end this nightmare one way or another.

Trembling, Gunomoy walked the lonely road to the dilapidated warehouse. As he peered into its shadowy maw, part of him hoped never to emerge again. Steeling himself, he stepped inside to face his destiny.

But would he find salvation, or a fate far worse than death within those walls? The conclusion to this twisted game was drawing near, and only one would make it out alive.

Gunomoy stepped slowly into the gloom of the old warehouse. His eyes strained to adjust as dread squeezed his heart.

"Welcome, Gunomoy," came Siddhartha's smooth voice from the darkness. Gunomoy spun around but couldn't locate him.

"Come out where I can see you!" Gunomoy said, hating the tremor in his voice.

Siddhartha emerged from the shadows with a theatrical flourish. "No need for panic, my friend. I merely wanted a word."

Gunomoy eyed the man warily. "What more could you possibly want from me?"

Siddhartha smiled that bone-chilling smile. "All I want are the secrets buried inside you. But you've been... resistant to share. I thought a more personal setting might relax your inhibitions."

Gunomoy shuddered. The warehouse's isolated location meant no one would hear his screams.

"Please, just let me go," he begged. "I'll do anything."

Siddhartha tilted his head, regarding Gunomoy with mock sympathy. "Now now, where would be the fun in that? No, we're just getting started unpeeling the layers. Tell me Gunomoy, what is your deepest, darkest sin?"

Gunomoy wracked his brain for anything to placate this madman without endangering himself further. In a trembling voice he confessed to minor theft as a child.

Siddhartha sighed dramatically. "Come now, surely you have more sordid tales than that. I can see the guilt and shame writhing beneath your skin, begging to be released. Unburden yourself to me, Gunomoy, and find absolution."

Gunomoy shook violently, but held his silence. Siddhartha's eyes flashed with anger at being denied. This game was escalating far beyond either of their control, and only one would make it out alive. But which one's fate was sealed?

The temperature in the warehouse seemed to plummet as Siddhartha stared down Gunomoy with naked rage.

"It seems you've left me no choice," he said in a low, threatening voice. "If you won't open up willingly, I'll pry the truth from your cold, dead lips."

Gunomoy backed away in fear, but Siddhartha was too quick. He lunged with an animalistic growl, tackling Gunomoy to the ground. They grappled violently, Siddhartha slowly gaining the upper hand in his madness-fueled strength.

Gunomoy scrabbled desperately for anything to defend himself with as Siddhartha's hands closed around his throat. Through watering eyes, he spotted a rusted iron pipe on the floor and swung it with all his might.

There was a sickening crunch and Siddhartha slumped, blood pouring from a massive head wound. Gunomoy crawled free on hands and knees, gasping for air. He stared in shock at Siddhartha's lifeless body, realizing with dread what he had done.

In that moment, all the fear and anxiety came crashing down on Gunomoy at once. He let out an anguished wail that echoed through the lonely warehouse. What would he do now? How could he live with the guilt of taking another's life, even in self defense?

As dusk fell, Gunomoy emerged dazed and blood-spattered from the warehouse of horrors. With trembling hands, he called the police and confessed everything with a dead, hollow voice. Now he could only await his fate, and pray for forgiveness from a higher power for the darkness that dwelled within.

The game was over, but the shadows it cast would haunt Gunomoy forever more. In the end, perhaps they all lost their humanity within those walls. The only question left was what came next, for a man who had gazed into the abyss of his own capacity for violence.

The Clock is Ticking

Shruti checked her watch as she hurried down the empty streets of Kolkata. It was 10:45pm, just 15 minutes until curfew. In the 8 weeks since the first murder, the city had grown increasingly paranoid. A strict dusk till dawn curfew was imposed in hopes of catching the killer who, like clockwork, struck once a week at exactly 11pm.

As Assistant Commissioner of Police, Shruti had been working tirelessly to solve the case. But without new leads, the killer remained ominously elusive. Tonight, Shruti was leaving the station later than usual, having lost track of time pouring over case files.

Shruti picked up her pace, her heels clicking urgently against the pavement. As she rounded the corner, a dark figure emerged from the shadows. Before she could react, a cloth was pressed firmly over her mouth. She struggled against her attacker's iron grip but quickly felt her body grow weak as the chloroform took hold. The last thing she saw was her watch display 11pm before everything went black.

Shruti awoke with a start, her head pounding. As her vision cleared she realized with horror that she was chained by her wrists to a cold cement wall. The room was barely lit save for a single naked bulb above her head. Shruti tugged desperately at her bindings but to no avail.

"Look who's finally joined us," a voice snarled from the darkness. A figure emerged, their face hidden behind a grotesque mask. "The infamous Assistant Commissioner, my special guest of honor. It seems the clock has struck 11..."

"Why are you doing this?" Shruti demanded, trying to mask the fear in her voice.

The killer tilted their head, as if pondering the question. "Justice must be served. An eye for an eye, a tooth for a tooth. These people, they're all the same. Corrupt, vile criminals who think they can get away with anything. But I know the truth, and now they're paying for their sins."

Shruti's mind raced, piecing together the killer's cryptic words. Could the murders be vigilante hits on criminals the legal system had failed to punish? If so, that would explain the meticulously planned nature of the crimes.

"I can help you," Shruti said, keeping her tone calm yet urgent. "Let me go and I promise I'll look into your allegations. But killing won't solve anything - it will only lead to more death."

The killer let out a mirthless laugh. "Help? From someone like you, part of the very system that lets evil fester? No, it's far too late for that now. You'll serve as my final masterpiece, the pièce de résistance that will really send a message. Then true justice will be done."

With that, the killer turned and left Shruti alone with her churning thoughts and dwindling hope. She had no idea how long she'd been unconscious - hours perhaps, leaving her with little time before the killer's deadline. Shruti scanned her surroundings frantically, but there was nothing within reach that could aid her escape. She was trapped with a madman, and the clock was ticking.

As the minutes crept by with excruciating slowness, Shruti's mind recalled the key details of each previous murder. She knew that somehow, the victims were linked - but what was the connection? Their identities, ages, and profiles appeared entirely random on paper. Yet the killer spoke of punishing criminals - could their transgressions be buried deeper, lost to official records?

Suddenly, an old case from Shruti's past resurfaced in her memory. Years ago, when she was a fresh-faced recruit, there had been allegations of police corruption surrounding an unsolved string of burglaries. Powerful figures were said to be involved in covering up the true culprits' identities. At the time, Shruti's superiors shut the investigation down, declaring the matter closed. But what if it was never really closed at all?

A plan started forming in Shruti's mind. If she could get the killer to reveal more, to validate her theory was correct, it may be leverage to bargain for her freedom. Though the risk was great, it was her only hope.

As if on cue, heavy footsteps approached once more. "Time to begin," the killer said ominously, brandishing a rusted blade. Shruti steeled her nerves.

"Wait," she said, her voice steady. "Before you do anything, tell me - were you the one behind those burglaries years ago? The ones the higher-ups helped sweep under the rug?"

Even through the mask, Shruti sensed the killer's surprise at her question. A tense silence followed before they responded. "So the great Assistant Commissioner put it together after all. Yes, it was me. My friends and I needed money for our sick mother's medical bills. But when the rich and powerful found out, they didn't like the bad press. So they paid off your superiors to pin it on some poor scapegoats while the real criminals walked free. It seems even you were just a puppet back then."

Shruti nodded slowly, processing this confirmation. "I believe you. And you're right, the system failed us both. But killing won't undo that wrong - it will only breed more anger and suffering. Let me help you get justice the right way. Release me, and I promise to reopen the case. We can arrest those truly responsible together, legally this time."

The killer hesitated, Considering Shruti's proposition. After an agonizing minute, they responded. "You have 48 hours. If I don't hear on the news that the investigation is underway by then, your time will be up." With that, they unlocked Shruti's restraints and vanished back into the darkness without another word.

Rubbing her sore wrists, Shruti fled the desolate building as fast as her exhausted body could carry her. Outside, the first light of dawn was just beginning to spread across the sky. She had survived, but her work was only beginning. True to her word, Shruti raced directly to her office and called an emergency press conference. There, she revealed the killer's allegations and announced a full reinvestigation of the decade old burglary case. Orders were given to haul in all suspects, including certain notable figures, for questioning.

Two days later, headlines blared of several high-level arrests as damning new evidence emerged. It seemed the killer's version of events held disturbing truth that had long festered in the shadows. That night, as Shruti watched the eleven o'clock news recap from the safety of her home, she breathed a long sigh of relief. Justice had been served - fully and correctly, this time around. The killers' deadly game had come to an end, and perhaps some small measure of peace could now be found by all.

The Red Bike

Shaan woke with a start, his sheets drenched in sweat. Another night, another blackout. He sat up slowly, his head pounding, and glanced at the clock - it was 3am. He tried to remember what had happened last night but there was nothing, just darkness. The same darkness that had plagued him for the past 6 months.

Every few weeks or so, he would simply lose time with no explanation or memory of what transpired. The spells were unpredictable and disorienting. Doctors had run test after test but found nothing physically wrong. It was as if someone was erasing pieces of his life without a trace. All he was left with was a vague image of a red bicycle with a worn white basket and muddy tires. Why this bike kept appearing in his fragmented thoughts, he did not know.

Shaan dragged himself to the bathroom and splashed water on his face, studying his exhausted reflection in the mirror. Dark circles had taken up permanent residence under his eyes. He was 34 but lately felt 74. This latest blackout had left him especially rattled - he could swear there was a new scratch on his forearm but had no idea how it got there.

Shaan brewed a strong pot of coffee and stepped outside for some fresh air, hoping the morning sun might lift his spirits. But as he opened the front door, he froze in shock. Leaning casually against the house was a dirty red bicycle, an exact match to the one in his visions. He stumbled backwards, clutching his head as a wave of dizziness washed over him. How was this possible? Was he losing his grip on reality?

Heart pounding, Shaan cautiously approached the strange bike, half expecting it to disappear in a puff of smoke. But it remained solid under his touch. With trembling hands, he rifled through the basket, uncovering a soggy newspaper and wallet. His wallet. Shaan tore it open to find his driver's license staring back at him, along with 500 cash. A rush of confusion and panic gripped him - had he been riding this bike last night during his blackout? Is that how the money and scratch got there?

He wheeled the creaky red bicycle inside, too wired to process what it could mean. As the sun rose higher, Shaan paced his small home restlessly, replaying the puzzle over and over in his mind. Finally, he knew he had to take action before descending further down the rabbit hole of his fragmented existence. He pulled out his laptop and began researching everything he could find about amnesia, dissociative disorders, fugue states - anything that could shed light on his plight.

Hours passed in an internet-fueled daze until one article caught Shaan's attention - a support group was holding a meeting that very night for people experiencing "non-epileptic seizure disorders." He had dismissed such support groups before as too problematic to tackle on his sporadic schedule. But deep down, Shaan was desperate for guidance and comfort from those who might truly understand the helplessness of living life at the mercy of unknown forces.

That evening, he entered the fluorescent-lit church hall with trepidation, steeling himself against potential judgment from clear-minded peers. But to his relief, the circle of folding chairs held a motley assortment of lost souls - some shaking, others disconnected, all painfully aware of an internal disruption beyond their control.

Shaan found a seat in the back and listened intently as people recounted experiences far stranger than his own - missing days traveling to foreign countries, entire identities fabricated for weeks at a time before crashing back to reality. As the sharing continued, he was startled to notice a familiar bicycle parked outside - the red bike, now rusted and beaten down by time. Could its owner be among this displaced group? Shaan hung back after the meeting, intercepting a disheveled man packing up craft supplies into a basket disturbingly like the one from his visions.

"Excuse me, I was wondering if that's your bicycle out there? It just seems very similar to one I've...seen before," Shaan asked apprehensively. The man studied him for a long moment before recognition flickered in his eyes. "My goodness, you must be Shaan. I'm Bill. I knew this day would come eventually, though I hoped it wouldn't be for a good while longer."

Shaan stepped back in confusion. "I'm sorry, have we met? Because I definitely don't remember -"

"No, you wouldn't remember," Bill sighed. "But we're connected whether we like it or not, thanks to this cursed condition. Come, let me buy you a coffee and I'll do my best to explain..."

Over strong espressos, Bill launched into a bewildering tale - one that made Shaan question if he was still locked in some dream. It seemed that over 15 years prior, the two had been close childhood friends, nearly inseparable on their bikes exploring the tangled oak forests near their small country town.

But one hot summer day while playing hide and seek, Shaan had suffered his first undocumented blackout - emerging hours later completely unaware of who Bill was or their history together. In the years that followed, Shaan's condition progressed to losing whole weeks at a time, each spell more harrowing than the last as his memories disintegrated like ash.

Meanwhile, Bill had desperately tried to jog his friend's slipping memory using their beloved bikes, to no avail. Eventually he too had begun experiencing fragments of lost time, often finding himself in distant places with no knowledge of how he got there. Doctors initially diagnosed a shared psychosis before conceding that the condition's cause and effects largely eluded modern science.

All these years later, it seemed like their fates remained tragically intertwined through that same antique red bicycle - the last remaining anchor from the innocent life they once knew. While Shaan strained to accept such a far-fetched story, everything Bill said resonated with some deeper knowing within, like recalling a dream just out of conscious reach.

Suddenly, he understood why the bike had become a talisman in his madness - it was a final thread tethering him to the reality that others remembered even if he no longer could. Shaan had so many questions, but Bill offered few concrete answers to their mysterious affliction beyond one hope - that by reconnecting, they could perhaps stave off further solitary unraveling and hold each other accountable through whatever challenges lay ahead.

It was a lot for Shaan to process in one sitting, but he knew he was not alone in this strangest of battles anymore. And if there was even a sliver of truth to Bill's connection from their stolen youth, he felt compelled to cling to any familiarity now floating to the surface before slipping away again, gods know when.

From that day forward, the two began relying on each other as conditions fluctuated and support systems shifted like quick sand. They traded contact details for emergencies, alerting relatives if spells extended beyond concerning limits. Simple strategies like greeting each visit with a code word helped validate identities were intact, guarding against the confusion that predators could exploit from damaged minds.

Gradually, bits of Shaan's shared history with Bill have begun resurfacing too - patchy memories like glimpses through a rain spattered window. Cycling the same trails they rode as kids seems to stir some recognition, as do photos of school feasts and football matches relegated to cardboard boxes in attics. He now understood how the red bicycle had been attempting to trigger those same nostalgic glimpses across the years, acting as a beacon whenever his friend felt unmoored.

While Shaan may never regain all that was stolen by his strange malady, knowing he wasn't truly alone in its effects brought immense comfort. And although the future remained shrouded in uncertainty, at least facing it alongside Bill felt far less terrifying than being lost to its murky whims without guide or compass. Now whenever that rusted red bike appeared in dreams or daytime visions, it was no longer a grim harbinger of fragmented existence - instead, a symbol that the solace of friendship can restore hope even to the most bewildering enigmas of the human experience.

The Visions in Sleep

Rehaan tossed and turned as they tried to sleep. It was the third night this week that they had lain awake, afraid to close their eyes. But their exhaustion was weighing heavy and sleep took them against their will.

As soon as dreams claimed consciousness, the visions began. Rehaan stood on a crowded city street, bustling with late evening activity. The atmosphere was lively but an underlying unease permeated the air. Their eyes were immediately drawn to a man standing at a street corner, face pale in the orange glow of streetlights.

A screech of tires broke the quiet chatter and a swerve of headlights blinded the crowd momentarily. As sights returned, panic and screams echoed in place of earlier merriment. A car had mounted the sidewalk, its bumper mere inches from the man. But he stood unmoving, unaware, as the vehicle barreled towards him.

Rehaan tried to shout, to wave their arms, anything to warn the unfortunate soul. But their voice was trapped inside, hands frozen at their sides. All they could do was watch in horror as the car collided with its target. On impact, the man's body folded under the force with a sickening crunch before being thrown aside like a ragdoll.

As onlookers rushed towards the victim, Rehaan jolted awake drenched in a cold sweat. Their heart thundered in their chest while raspy breaths fought to calm frayed nerves. The images were seared into their mind, more vivid and real than any dream. But they were just dreams, right? Visions imagined from an overactive mind under stress.

Rehaan decided a therapist may help alleviate their growing anxiety over these nightly terrors. After researching doctors in their area, they made an appointment with a Dr. Rhea Bakshi, a psychologist with two decades of experience in treating patients with dissociative disorders and trauma.

Their first session, Rehaan recounted the succession of vivid dreams that had plagued their nights for weeks. Dr. Bakshi listened intently, taking notes as Rehaan described each gruesome detail.

"I understand this has been frightening and distressing. However, there are a few elements that concern me." said the doctor. "The clarity and realism of the dreams is unusual. And the fact you seem to be experiencing them as an outside observer rather than a participant raises questions. Dissociative experiences can sometimes provide a glimpse into events outside our normal perception of time and space."

Rehaan was taken aback. They had come expecting reassurance that overactive imagination was to blame, not speculative theories about extrasensory phenomena.

"I know it's an extraordinary claim," continued Dr. Bakshi. "But given your character and lack of any psychiatric history, hypothesizing dissociative abilities warrants consideration over dismissing your experiences outright."

She suggested some relaxation and grounding techniques to help Rehaan manage their stress and disrupt unwanted visions. Dr. Bakshi also offered hypnotherapy to aid in exploring the dreams from a place of calm rather than fear. Rehaan agreed, wanting answers even if they challenged conventional beliefs.

That night, calm enveloped Rehaan as practiced mindfulness allowed dreamless sleep. The respite was welcome but brief, as vivid imagery soon permeated rest once more. This time, Rehaan stood in a suburban home, following muffled shouts down the hall. Pushing open a bedroom door, they bore witness to a lover's quarrel turned deadly.

A wife lay crumpled on the ground while her enraged husband towered above, fist still clenched from the final beating. Chest heaving, he glanced around the room in panic before his crazed eyes landed on Rehaan, unseeing. Stumbling past in shock, Rehaan stared in horror at the corpse, memorizing each gruesome detail though wishing to unsee it all.

The next session, Rehaan's distress was palpable as they recounted the fresh nightmare. Dr. Bakshi listened intently before speaking.

"I understand this is difficult to accept. However, given what you've described, I believe we are dealing with something beyond imagination here. It seems you may have an undiagnosed ability to witness traumatic events at a distance, though the mechanism remains unclear. I'd like to conduct a hypnotherapy session to see if we can gain insight into what's happening."

Rehaan agreed, desperate for answers even if it meant entertaining notions outside accepted norms of reality. That Friday, they arrived at Dr. Bakshi's office ready to confront whatever mysteries lay beneath the disturbing visions.

Under hypnosis, Dr. Bakshi guided Rehaan back to the dreams, encouraging them to recall every minute detail without fear or judgment. Images from the city street and suburban home resurfaced vividly, as if Rehaan was living them anew.

Dr. Bakshi then asked probing questions - about sensations, thoughts, feelings experienced in those moments. Slowly, insights began to surface. Rehaan spoke of visceral emotions that were not their own, knowledge of events they had no way of knowing.

It was in that trance state that the incredible, impossible truth began to take shape. Somehow, through what force or faculty none could say, Rehaan was experiencing genuine visions of real tragedies taking place elsewhere, viewing them as a disassociated observer beyond the normal bounds of space and time.

The hypnotherapy sessions continued, uncovering more about Rehaan's rare gift and the profound responsibilities it carried. With patience and guidance, they learned to harness rather than fear their ability, carefully using it to provide solace and even aid investigations when possible.

While questions remained around how and why such a faculty existed, Rehaan took comfort knowing they were not alone. With Dr. Bakshi's care and insight, they embraced their dissociative experiences and dedicated themselves to the service of preventing further injustice in this odd, wonderful way.

After the startling revelations of the hypnosis sessions, Rehaan began keeping a detailed diary of any night visions that came to them. With Dr. Bakshi's help, they learned meditation techniques to induce self-hypnosis and explore these trances with more clarity.

In one such session, Rehaan revisited a dream of a boating accident that had occurred a month prior. Through focused questioning, they were able to recall distinguishing details like the location, make of boat, and description of one passenger.

Dr. Bakshi surreptitiously looked into recent incidents matching the details. To their amazement, she found news reports of an accident that played out exactly as Rehaan described, right down to a unique tattoo borne by one of the survivors.

This confirmed, beyond any doubt, that Rehaan was truly experiencing real events from afar through their dissociated state. With great responsibility came greater exploration. Under Dr. Bakshi's guidance, Rehaan began using self-hypnosis deliberately to seek out clues that could help close cases that stumped investigators.

In one instance, Rehaan's visions helped identify a fire that was ruled an accident but later proven to be arson and insurance fraud. On another, they provided key details that linked a missing child to an unemployed neighbor secretly struggling with dark desires.

While Rehaan's abilities remained an enigma, they found solace and purpose serving justice in this unique way. And through their work with Dr. Bakshi, they came to understand themselves not as "gifted" but simply different - with dissociative experiences to steward rather than stigmatize or fear.

The Forgotten Sketchbook

Shukhen Biswas sighed as he slid his key into the front door of his small apartment after a long day at the office. It had been another grueling week of meetings, reports, and late nights trying to meet deadlines. As the Director of Marketing for a large tech company, the job provided a stable paycheck but left little time for much else these days.

As Shukhen entered his home, he slipped off his shoes by the door and made a beeline for the fridge. Grabbing a cold beer, he settled onto the worn couch and gazed absentmindedly around the room. his eyes paused on a bookshelf in the corner that had once housed his collection of interests from years past - books on art history, travel guides of faraway lands, photography how-tos. But over time, the shelves had grown sparse and dusty as other priorities took over.

One faded blue object caught Shukhen's attention amidst the bare wood. He walked over and gently lifted it - his old sketchbook, buried and forgotten these past few years under the pressures of corporate life. Opening the cover, he turned the first crisp page and froze. Where half-finished pencil sketches of landscapes and cityscapes had once been, polished ink drawings now inhabited the spaces. But these were not

Shukhen's own works. The style was different, more detailed and refined.

Shukhen racked his brain, trying to make sense of what he was seeing. These drawings were certainly not done by his own hand. He flipped through more pages, each one now complete with intricate illustrations that felt like something from the pages of an art magazine. Becoming uneasy, he closed the sketchbook and placed it back on the shelf.

After a restless night's sleep, Shukhen decided to look further into the mystery. He meticulously went through each page of the sketchbook again, studying the techniques and subjects of the finished drawings for any clues. The styles varied - some captured lush jungle scenes, others portraits of people from different ethnicities and time periods. Most were landscapes or animals, but interspersed were surreal images that seemed otherworldly.

As Shukhen examined an impressionistic drawing of rolling grassy hills, something caught his eye in the bottom right corner. Written in fine cursive was a signature - A. Jones. Could this be the artist responsible for the completed works? Eager to find answers, Shukhen spent the rest of the day researching the signature online to no avail. No artists named A. Jones matched the styles he had seen. He began to wonder if this was all just an elaborate trick of the mind.

That evening, Shukhen decided to clear his head with a walk through the park near his apartment. The sun was setting, casting long shadows across the grounds. As he strolled past a grove of trees, a figure emerged from the dusk. An older woman was sitting on a bench, softly sketching the scenery with pencil and paper. Her salt and pepper hair was cropped short, and fine wrinkles lined her kind face. Something about her demeanor seemed familiar to Shukhen.

"Pardon me, I couldn't help but notice your sketching. You have a wonderful talent," Shukhen said kindly.

The woman looked up and smiled. "Why thank you! Drawing has always been my passion. I'm Anne, pleased to meet you."

Shukhen froze. "Anne...Anne Jones?"

A puzzled expression crossed the woman's face. "Yes, how did you know?"

With shaking hands, Shukhen opened their sketchbook to a random page, turning it toward Anne. "Because I think you finished all these drawings in my book. But that's impossible, it was locked away for years..."

Anne gasped softly as she stared at the illustration. "This...this is my work. But I have never seen this sketchbook before in my life! There must be some explanation..."

The two sat discussing far into the night, but no logical solution presented itself. Anne swore she had never met Shukhen or seen the sketchbook until that moment. Yet her signature and unmistakable style filled its pages. They decided the only path was to dig further.

The next day, Anne shared old sketches and portfolios from throughout her long career. Shukhen cross-referenced the styles to be absolutely certain - it was a perfect match. They reviewed all the subjects in Shukhen's book to see if any held special significance. One stood out - a scene of ruins deep in a jungle that neither had seen before.

"These could be a real place that holds the key," Shukhen declared. After searching satellite maps and archaeology journals, they discovered the ruins were located in a remote region of Costa Rica. Without any other leads, Shukhen resolved to travel there in hopes of finding resolution to the mystery.

After an grueling multi-day trek through thick jungle trails, Shukhen arrived exhausted but determined at the ruins. Moss-covered stone structures emerged from the dense foliage, more overgrown than expected. As he cleared vines away, Shukhen noticed strange etchings on the crumbling walls. The markings resembled symbols from the dreamlike pictures in the sketchbook.

At that moment, a rustling came from behind. Shukhen whirled around to find Anne emerging from the undergrowth, out of breath. "I had a hunch you may find answers here, so I chartered a plane. Please, let me help."

Together they uncovered more of the ruin, noting similarities between architectural features and illustrations. Deeper in the jungle, a carved staircase led underground. Shukhen and Anne descended with trepidation into the dark, torchlight flickering off ancient drawings that lined the earthen walls.

At the bottom, they discovered a small chamber. In the center stood a plain stone tablet, etched all over with the same strange pictographs. Shukhen pulled out the sketchbook and compared the images - it was a perfect match. A gasp arose from Anne as her eyes fell upon unusual symbols in one corner of the tablet, identical to her forgotten signature.

"It's as if this place tapped into my subconscious and communicated these images through your book across time and space," Anne said breathlessly. "These ruins must hold some anomalous psychic property we don't fully understand. The mysteries of the world continue to surprise me, even in my old age."

Shukhen nodded slowly, piecing together the unbelievable sequence of events. They had unearthed an extraordinary phenomenon that explained the unsolvable enigma. Though the questions outnumbered the answers, one truth was clear - this chance meeting had led them to uncover something literally beyond imagination. Shukhen smiled, grateful for the unforeseen journey that reminded us that wonders still exist beyond our comprehension. As long as there are sketchbooks to fill, the possibilities are endless.

The Spare Room Guest

Rajiv browsed through the listings on Airbnb, reviewing the kinds of spare rooms and guest houses people in his neighborhood were renting out. As a science teacher at the local high school, the pay was decent but things were tight financially. He dreamed of taking a sabbatical to travel through Europe like he had planned years ago, before responsibilities took over his life. That's when he had an idea - why not rent out his spare room and use the extra income to start saving for his grand trip?

His room wasn't anything fancy but it was clean, comfortable and private. He added some photos and wrote a description highlighting the room's amenities and proximity to public transit. Within days he had his first booking for a solo female traveler coming into town on business. Tanya seemed nice over messages and checked in smoothly when she arrived. Rajiv gave her a quick tour then left her to settle in, only interacting when their paths crossed in the kitchen. She was quiet but polite. By the end of her five night stay, Rajiv had made over $500 after Airbnb's fees. This could really work, he thought excitedly.

More guests followed, each leaving glowing reviews of the comfortable accommodations and Rajiv's hospitality. He was developing a good reputation on the platform. Then one weekend, he received a booking for the entire following week from a man named Robert. In his profile pic, Robert looked utterly nondescript - middle aged, average build, short brown hair. His profile said he was in town on "personal travel" but provided no other details. Rajiv didn't give it much thought, just confirming the details and cleaning the room extra thoroughly before Robert's arrival.

The first couple nights were uneventful. Robert kept to himself as Rajiv had with previous guests. But on the third night, Rajiv was woken from his sleep by banging and thumps coming from the spare room. Frightened, he grabbed the baseball bat he kept by his bed and crept down the hall, pressing his ear to the door. All went silent. He waited, then knocked gently. "Everything ok in there?" More silence. Figuring it was nothing, Rajiv went back to bed uneasy.

The next morning, Rajiv went to the kitchen to make coffee and found Robert already up, fully dressed at this early hour. "Morning," Rajiv said cautiously, eyeing the man. Robert just grunted in response, staring into space. As Rajiv poured his coffee, he noticed Robert's door was wide open. He glanced in, half expecting to see signs of a struggle from whatever had happened last night. But the room was perfectly tidy, almost sterilely so. Confused, Rajiv decided not to probe further and risk upsetting his guest.

Over the next few days, strange noises continued coming from Robert's room at odd hours - crashes, thumps, whispers. Rajiv began worrying for his safety but didn't want to jump to conclusions or get the police involved without cause. He left extra baked goods by Robert's door to appear unintimidated but stayed in his own room at night with the bat close by. On the final night of Robert's stay, Rajiv heard manic laughter mixed with sobs through the wall. Gripped with terror, he called out to the man pleadingly, "Sir, are you alright in there? Do you need help?" The laughter cut off abruptly. Everything went eerily still.

The next morning, Rajiv found Robert already packed and waiting stone-faced by the front door, bags in tow. "Thanks for the stay," Robert stated flatly, handing over an envelope stuffed with cash before bailing swiftly without another word. Rajiv was relieved to see him go but something felt desperately off about the whole strange visit. Looking in the spare room, it appeared untouched except for a new smell that hung faintly in the air - something floral yet acrid that made Rajiv's skin crawl. He hastily aired the place out, scrubbing vigorously to banish any trace of Robert.

In the following weeks, Rajiv messaged Airbnb repeatedly to have Robert's profile removed but they refused without a compelling safety complaint. His nightmares were plagued by Robert's pallid visage and his manic cackles in the night. Things went back to normal for a while with pleasant guests until one review popped up that stopped Rajiv in his tracks - it was from Robert, praising the "private retreat" and "thoughtful host". Fearfully, Rajiv checked the calendar - there were no upcoming bookings from Robert listed but he couldn't shake the feeling that the strange man was not through with him yet.

Months passed with no incidents and Rajiv had almost convinced himself it was all in his head, that first house sitting just went awry somehow. But one night in July, everything changed. Rajiv heard a click at the front door at 3am, waking with a start. Spying out his bedroom window, he saw a figure shuffling up the front steps under the pale moonlight - unmistakably Robert. How did he get in?! Terrified, Rajiv dialed 911 immediately as Robert began slamming into the front door, jiggling the knob maniacally while shrieking "Let me in! Let me back in!" Within minutes, police cars pulled up with sirens wailing. Officers apprehended a raging Robert, sedating him after a struggle.

In the aftermath, Rajiv learned Robert had broken into multiple prior tenants' homes across the country claiming to be "chosen" by the spirits living there. A thorough background check found he had a long history of severe mental illness, frequently going off his meds. Although Rajiv wished to press charges, he was talked down by the police - it would be a battle not worth fighting and could further endanger him. Airbnb was also gravely apologetic, removing Robert's account and personally following up to ensure Rajiv's safety going forward.

Shaken but ultimately unharmed, Rajiv decided to take a permanent break from hosting strangers, at least for now. Maybe one day when he felt truly ready again, he'd give Airbnb another shot to supplement his Europe fund. But for the time being, his spare room would stay just that - a sanctuary purely for himself and those he knew well. The lesson was clear: you never truly know who might come knocking in the night when you open your private spaces to the unpredictable public online. Some doors are better left closed until you can be sure what might wait beyond.

About the Author

Sayan Panda

Sayan Panda, a talented author hailing from the vibrant city of Kolkata, has captivated readers with his imaginative storytelling. With a background in English literature and a passion for the written word, Panda has established himself as a noteworthy voice in the literary world. Having already published six books across various genres, he now ventures into unexplored territory, delving into the realms of the paranormal and the macabre. This foray into the mysterious and eerie showcases Panda's versatile storytelling abilities and his willingness to push the boundaries of his craft. Alongside his writing endeavors, Panda also dedicates himself to educating young minds as a dedicated school teacher.

www.ingramcontent.com/pod-product-compliance
Lightning Source LLC
LaVergne TN
LVHW041557070526
838199LV00046B/2017